Jake Greenthumb

To Brent—Loki
To Michelle and Nelson—J.G.

For information contact:
MONDO Publishing
980 Avenue of the Americas
New York, NY 10018
Visit our web site at http://www.mondopub.com

Printed in the United States of America
02 03 04 05 06 07 08 HC 9 8 7 6 5 4 3 2 1
02 03 04 05 06 07 08 PB 9 8 7 6 5 4 3 2 1

ISBN 1-59034-186-4 (hardcover)   ISBN 1-59034-037-X (pbk.)

Designed by Ed Miller

Library of Congress Cataloging-in-Publication Data

Loki.
   Jake Greenthumb / by Loki ; illustrated by Jason Gaillard.
      p. cm.
   Summary: Because he is good with plants, Jake receives so many plants from his
neighbors that they take over his room.
   ISBN 1-59034-186-4 -- ISBN 1-59034-037-X (pbk.)
   [1. Plants--Fiction.] I. Gaillard, Jason, ill. II. Title.

PZ7.L83115 Jak 2002
[E]--dc21

2001054448

Jake Greenthumb

by Loki

Illustrated by Jason Gaillard

MONDO

Jake Greenthumb could make anything grow. His neighbors were always asking him to take care of their plants.

4

On Monday, Mr. Vine gave Jake an ivy plant that would not climb.

On Wednesday, the ivy was climbing and climbing.

On Thursday, Officer Peel gave Jake an orange tree that would not grow oranges.

On Saturday, the orange
tree was full of oranges.

8

On Sunday, Mrs. Thorn's cactus lost its prickles.

On Monday, Sally's sunflowers were brown.

9

On Tuesday, Dr. Cone's pine tree just would not grow.

10

Some days, it seemed like everyone in town had a plant for Jake.

And Jake took them all. Oh boy, *did* he!

11

And all the plants took up more and more of Jake's bedroom. Oh boy, *did* they!

12

Jake's mom told him again and again that one day the house would turn into a jungle.

Jake knew his mom was kidding. Nothing like that could really happen . . . could it?

One morning, when Jake was watering the banana tree, his socks got wet in the mud.

Mud?

Huh?

Jake always kept his room
clean. You could ask anyone. Really.

But there it was—*mud*.

Very strange.

16

Jake pulled his socks off and let
the mud squish between his toes.
It felt good. Still, he'd better clean
it up before Mom saw.

17

Jake headed to the bathroom for an old towel to clean up the mess. But—wait a minute! Where was the bathroom? It was right here the last time he looked. Wasn't it? Very strange!

19

Jake looked and looked, but he could not find the bathroom. It was not behind the sunflowers or under the orange tree.

The bathroom was not under the palm or in the ivy.

Jake looked and looked. He looked in this plant. He looked under that plant. He looked everywhere. The bathroom was not there. It was gone—*just gone*.

Now, Jake was smart enough to know that this would not make his mother happy. He sat down on a patch of grass to think.

What to do, what to do . . ? Jake knew how to make plants *grow*. But how to make them *go* . . . that was a tricky one.

Jake thought and thought and thought some more.

Just then, there was
a knock at the door.
It was Sally.

Suddenly, Jake had an idea.
He grabbed the sunflowers . . .

. . . and threw open the door.

"Hello, Sally!" Jake said. He grinned and handed Sally the bright yellow sunflowers.

"Oh, they are beautiful! You're my hero!" Sally cried.

Jake spent the rest of the
morning bringing plants back
to his neighbors.

Mr. Vine was happy.

Officer Peel was happy.

28

Mrs. Thorn was happy.

Dr. Cone was happy.

29

Whew! Giving all of those plants back to the people they came from was tiring, but now everyone was happy . . . well, almost everyone.

Now everyone was happy!